Will the Real Ike Hanson Please Stand Up?

It's all here! Learn about your favorite Hanson brother, Clarke Isaac Hanson!

★ How does he deal with his success?
★ What makes him really get serious?
★ What does he do to make his friends laugh?
★ Could YOU be the perfect girl for him?

Find all these answers and more in . . .

Isaac Hanson: Totally Ike!

Look for other biographies from Archway Paperbacks

For orders other than by individual consumers, Pocket Books grants a discount on the purchase of **10 or more** copies of single titles for special markets or premium use. For further details, please write to the Vice-President of Special Markets, Pocket Books, 1633 Broadway, New York, NY 10019-6785, 8th Floor.

For information on how individual consumers can place orders, please write to Mail Order Department, Simon & Schuster Inc., 200 Old Tappan Road, Old Tappan, NJ 07675.

isaac hanson

TOTALLY IKE!
an unauthorized biography

nancy krulik

AN ARCHWAY PAPERBACK
Published by POCKET BOOKS
New York London Toronto Sydney Tokyo Singapore

AN ARCHWAY PAPERBACK *Original*

 An Archway Paperback published by
POCKET BOOKS, a division of Simon & Schuster Inc.
1230 Avenue of the Americas, New York, NY 10020

Copyright © 1998 by Nancy Krulik

ISBN: 0-671-02446-9

First Archway Paperback printing February 1998

10 9 8 7 6 5 4 3 2 1

AN ARCHWAY PAPERBACK and colophon are registered trademarks of Simon & Schuster Inc.

Front cover photo by Y. Lenquette/Retna

Printed in the U.S.A.

IL 5+

For my parents, who made sure there were always books and music in our house and in our hearts. Thanks!

—NEK

CONTENTS

isaac
hanson

WILL THE REAL ISAAC HANSON PLEASE STAND UP?

Clarke Isaac Hanson has been called the heart and soul of Hanson, the red-hot pop group he created with his younger brothers, Taylor and Zac. Fans consider Ike the most knowing member of Hanson, the one who is so sentimental that he names his guitars after the girls he likes. (His current guitar has no name, since Ike is still searching for his lady love.) He has a quiet confidence that makes him seem a lot more mature than his seventeen years. And although he can come across as slightly glum, Ike's fans agree that his moodiness is part of why they love him—he's a teenage rebel with a dark and brooding side.

But if you were to ask Ike Hanson to describe himself, the answer might surprise you. Isaac surely would reply that he was the "stupid, goofy" member of the band. And to prove it, Ike might break into his Kermit the Frog and Bullwinkle imitations. He also does a mean Beavis and Butt-head impersonation. That's the one that really cracks up his brothers, Taylor and Zac. (Heh heh heh . . . did we say *crack?*)

So who is the real Isaac Hanson? The answer is . . . all of the above. The eldest Hanson brother is very sensitive and can be kind of shy sometimes. On the other hand, he can also be a total goofball, making wacky faces for the television camera and fooling around with his brothers in the studio or backstage before a show.

One thing Ike takes very seriously is his music. His songs are his passion, and he believes wholeheartedly in his talent. It is that belief that carried him through all of the years Hanson struggled before the album *Middle of Nowhere* (and its number one single, "MMMBop") made them stars. For years, the *Billboard* charts were filled with angry alternative rock—and many producers felt that Hanson's positive, upbeat message just wouldn't connect with listeners. But Ike didn't change his musical style just to make record producers happy. He stuck with his own sound.

"We were always doing (the kind of music) we love to do," he told *MTV News*. "We weren't worrying about what other bands were doing. We do what we do. And they do what they do. Besides, there's enough hard stuff in life, plenty of stuff to get us down. For us, our music is a way to get away from things."

Isaac believes so strongly in his music that he doesn't even care what his critics say. "Some people make fun of Hanson," he admits with a shrug of his shoulders. "But I don't give a rip."

Still, even when he's talking about his beloved music, Ike can get very silly. When one reporter kept complimenting Ike on the music on *Middle of Nowhere,* Ike teased, "Too bad you can't marry (the album)!"

There is one thing Ike will *never* joke about, however, and that is the devotion of his fans. While his brothers may nickname the throngs of cheering girls "the screamers," Isaac takes the fans' devotion very seriously. "It's an honor. It's hard to believe that they are all there to hear us. We always want to give the fans their money's worth," he insists.

It's a good thing Ike is fond of his fans. After all, wherever he goes, they are sure to follow—to Tulsa, Tokyo, and the Middle of Nowhere (which just happens to be the title of Hanson's new behind-the-scenes video).

But despite all the fans, all the hit records, and all the sold-out concerts all over the world, Ike Hanson insists that he's really just a regular seventeen-year-old guy.

JUST YOUR AVERAGE KID

No, your eyes did not just deceive you. Ike Hanson really doesn't feel that he's all that different from other kids his age. Of course, most seventeen-year-olds don't travel all over the world, work with some of the best studio musicians and record producers, shoot music videos, or get chased wherever they go by screaming girls. But the truth is, Ike has managed to stay remarkably normal despite all the hoopla.

For starters, like many seventeen-year-olds, one of the things Isaac Hanson is most proud of is his newly minted driver's license. And someday, Ike plans on owning his dream car—a Corvette. (Sounds like every other seventeen-year-old guy you know, right?)

Now, with all the money Hanson has made from sales of records, videos, T-shirts, posters, key chains, and other items, you would think Ike could buy that car right now. But he hasn't. And that's because despite all of the fame and fortune, Ike has stayed true to the ethics that his parents, Walker and Diana Hanson, instilled in him at a very young age.

"Just because you earn a bit of money doesn't mean you have to buy a gigantoid house and fast cars," Ike says. "We'll probably put most of it in the bank. I'm sure we'll have better use for it when we're older."

At seventeen, Ike is a junior in high school. But Ike doesn't attend a regular high school. He and his brothers have always been home-schooled. But the fact that the Hansons are taught by their mother at home doesn't make them all that different from other kids in Oklahoma. The home-schooling movement has become quite large there. Some parents choose to teach their children at home for religious reasons. Others do it because they don't like the educational system in their area. It takes a huge commitment on the part of the parents who choose to home-school, but many feel the sacrifice is worth it. Diana Hanson has never publicly explained why she chose to home-school her children, but it was a plan that was already in motion long before Hansonmania broke out around the world. And as it turns out, the home-schooling comes in very handy, since it allows Ike and his brothers to stay on their school schedule while touring the world.

"We love home-schooling," Ike told *Seventeen* magazine. "It lets you focus on the things you enjoy."

Home-schooling also allows the boys to work their traveling into their curriculum. As Ike explained to a Tulsa reporter, "I think it's really neat to read about history-type stuff. We were reading about Winston Churchill when we were in England. History is cool when we're on tour, and in Europe we got to see all the things we normally only read about."

And how *about* all of that traveling? Hanson's touring schedule has taken the boys to Asia, Australia, and Europe, as well as cities across the United States. But has that changed Ike? No way! Of course, that's mostly because the Hanson brothers are used to living far from their Tulsa home. Even before the boys became famous, their father's job as an international executive for a Tulsa oil company meant that the family had to move to South America and the Caribbean for a year. Ike, Tay, and Zac lived in Ecuador, Venezuela, and Trinidad when they were younger.

"We're just back from Germany, ten days in the UK, five days in France, three in Germany, doing interviews with different magazines, TV, and radio," Ike told one Tulsa reporter. "We've lived all over the world, so the traveling we get to do now is fun, but it's not like we've never done it before."

Another thing Ike has in common with other seventeen-year-old guys is a passion for the girls. Unfortunately for Ike (but fortunately for all his fans), he hasn't been able to find that one special someone just yet.

"We're allowed to date," Ike told a *Teen Beat* reporter. "But no girlfriend would probably want to deal with our schedule."

And there's more good news for the millions of teenage girls out there who love Ike. He says he would date a fan—just not one who screamed every time he smiled at her. Of course, it's hard *not* to scream with excitement when Isaac stares at you with those big brown eyes. He's really gorgeous! And Ike works hard to keep himself looking great. For starters, like his brothers, he only orders diet soda in restaurants.

"Pop has a lot of sugar in it, and you know what that means," Tay told a reporter for *Rolling Stone* magazine.

"Pimples," Isaac chimed in. Ike's not alone in worrying about zits. Let's face it, pimples are an enemy every teen fights every day—even a hunk like Isaac Hanson!

Ike's hobbies are pretty much like any other teenager's. He loves skateboarding, street hockey, and Rollerblading. And on those rare nights when he gets a free second to turn on the tube, he tries to catch episodes of his favorite shows: *Frasier, Seinfeld, Beavis and Butt-head,* and *Men Behaving Badly.* Of course, before he can watch

TV, Isaac first has to help Taylor and Zac clean up the room they share in their Tulsa house (Ike and Tay share a bunk bed with Ike on top; Zac sleeps on a pull-out trundle). The guys' room often looks like a disaster area. (Sounds like just about every other teenage room, doesn't it?) But Ike's working on it.

"I'm trying to be neater," he promises. "Right now, our room looks like we trashed it—even though we haven't."

Another bad habit Ike's working on is biting his nails. And that's a habit he's got to break, because it affects his guitar playing. Luckily, Ike says he's finding the strength to resist the habit now.

Most importantly, Isaac Hanson has not fallen into any of the *really* bad habits that have become the pitfalls of pop stardom. He is still strongly anti-drugs, alcohol, and cigarettes.

"It's sad when bands get involved in things like that," Ike says.

Ike Hanson works very hard at staying the sweet, gentle guy he was before he got swept up in the whirlwind of success. Maybe that's why he gets so upset with people who say he's become different since Hanson became a household word. Still, Ike is realistic about the fact that people won't believe how little he's actually changed.

"We've had people say things like, 'Oh, the Hansons have changed,' but they haven't even seen us," Ike explains. "That's part of being in a band, though you learn to let it go. You can try to change their minds about what they might think, but most of the time, if you can't, you just don't worry about it."

That's right, Ike. You shouldn't worry about those few nasty critics. Millions of fans all over the world think you're great. And they're glad you've stayed as awesome and sweet as you've always been.

3

IN THE BEGINNING . . .

Maybe part of the reason Ike and his brothers have never gotten into that "star thing" is that their levelheaded parents would never allow them to become conceited jerks. Ike's parents, Walker and Diana Hanson, met in high school in Tulsa, Oklahoma. They shared an interest in music and a devout faith. Those combined interests led them to sing with a gospel group called the Horizons, performing in churches all over the country.

Eventually, Diana and Walker got married, and on November 17, 1980, they had their first child—a baby boy with light brown hair and soulful brown eyes. They named him Clarke Isaac, but everyone called him Ike (a nickname for his middle name, Isaac).

From day one, Diana and Walker sang to their

son. They serenaded him to sleep, coaxed him to eat through song, and had family sing-alongs while Walker played the guitar. Ike has strong memories of those early days.

"There was always singing and music around the house," Ike recalls. "My mom's been singing and listening to music ever since I could remember."

The Hanson family sing-alongs got a little larger on March 14, 1983, when blue-eyed, blond-haired Jordan Taylor Hanson (you probably call him Taylor or Tay) came along.

Ike and Tay are less than three years apart in age, and they have always been very close. They've shared a room in the Hanson family's Tulsa house since Tay was born. In 1985, that room became a little more crowded. Brown-eyed babe Zachary Walker Hanson joined the family on October 22 of that year.

Even before they could walk, the Hanson boys were singing. Walker taught them how to harmonize on the word "Amen" after saying grace at the dinner table. And to everyone's amazement, the boys' voices blended together perfectly. "It was the most natural thing in the world for us to sing together," Ike has said.

But the family's harmonious life in Tulsa was about to take a big jolt. Walker Hanson had moved up the ranks of an Oklahoma oil drilling and gas company called Helmerich and Payne. By 1989, he was the manager of the company's international administration. And that was a job that required relocating—to South America and the Carribean!

The move wasn't totally unexpected. Walker and Diana had always known that this was part of the territory when it came to Walker's job. Luckily, the boys didn't have to leave school for the move; home-schooled kids can learn anywhere. And so the Hanson family took off for a year of excitement, adventure, and education in Ecuador, Venezuela, and Trinidad and Tobago.

Living in new cultures can be exciting—and a little scary. While they were in South America and the Caribbean, the boys lived in camps run by Helmerich and Payne. That meant there were other U.S. kids around who knew about American culture and could speak English. There were also huge lizards, sharp-toothed crocodiles, bats, and rats in the camps.

Ike and his brothers felt they were lucky to live in South America. They could swim every day of the year—something most boys who live with Tulsa's snowbound winters can only dream about. And they had the wonderful opportunity to experience life in other cultures firsthand. This gave Ike and his brothers a natural curiosity about and tendency to respect other cultures, a trait that would come in handy during Hanson's world promotional tour of 1997.

Still, there was something the boys truly missed about living in Tulsa, and that was music.

Sure, there were radio stations in South America and the Caribbean, but none of them featured the Top 40 music the Hanson boys had grown up loving. Luckily, Diana and Walker had anticipated that problem and brought along a collection of Time-Life compilation tapes. The tapes were filled with rock-and-roll classics from the 1950s and '60s. It didn't take long for the boys to start singing along with tunes by Chuck Berry, Little Richard, Bobby Darrin, Aretha Franklin, and the Beatles. At night, Walker made sure the family kept up their sing-along tradition—only now the boys were singing the songs from the Time-Life tapes.

Isaac and his brothers developed a real love of old R&B (that's rhythm-and-blues) music while they were in South America. And to this day, they say that's the music that has influenced them the most.

By the time the family returned to Tulsa, the Hanson boys were ready for some new music. Of course, they listened to Top 40 on the radio, but they wanted something more. Ike and his brothers knew that the sound they were looking for didn't exist . . . *yet*. If the Hanson brothers wanted to hear the kind of music they were dreaming of, they would have to write it and sing it themselves. Which, of course, is exactly what they did.

☆ 4

MAKING MUSIC!

It would be hard for Hanson ever to record the very first songs Ike, Tay, and Zac wrote. That's because they never wrote them down. "At first, we didn't even write them out," Ike explains. "We just sang them."

Sang them and promptly forgot them, is more like it. And that soon became frustrating. So, by the time Ike was in third grade, he took it upon himself to start writing down the words and the music. Ike already could read music, having taken piano lessons since the age of five.

But back then, all of the composing and singing the boys did was just for fun. They never dreamed of performing in public—until one day when they went onstage at a Christmas party for their father's company.

The performance was completely spontaneous—the boys hadn't planned it or rehearsed for it. (Well, actually, they'd been rehearsing for it all their lives.) The audience at the party was instantly taken by the three a capella Hansons. *(A capella* means singing without being accompanied by instruments.) The boys got a standing ovation, and that was it. Ike and his brothers had been bitten by the performing bug—and there was no turning back now!

At first, Ike, Tay, and Zac called themselves the Hanson Brothers. (They later tried the Hansons, but they thought it sounded too much like the "Handsomes"—which would be appropriate but really corny!) Ike, Tay, and Zac immediately got started working up a real act. The boys performed wherever they could—at local parties and school gymnasiums. Their act consisted of the oldies they'd learned in South America.

"The first music we ever performed were fifties and sixties songs like 'Johnny B. Goode,' 'Rockin' Robin,' and 'Splish Splash,'" Ike recalls. "We were comfortable with them."

If you were to have seen the Hansons performing back then, you might not instantly recognize them as today's Hanson. Sure, Ike still had those deep, soulful brown eyes, Tay still had his signature smile, and Zac was as cute as ever, but back in the old days, the Hanson brothers wore matching tough-guy jeans jackets and dark sunglasses. And here comes a real shocker: they all had (gasp!) crew cuts.

But that's not the only difference in their performing styles. Early Hanson shows featured the guys performing self-choreographed dance routines.

"Back then, we weren't playing instruments, so we got to be a little more involved with the audience, coaxing them to dance and clap along with us, that sort of thing," Ike explains.

Little by little, the boys began making a name for themselves, and by 1992, they were asked to perform at the Mayfest, an annual arts festival in Tulsa. They performed for almost an hour, filling their fifteen-song set mostly with oldies but performing six original Hanson compositions as well. The brothers H didn't win the competition, but the audience clearly was amazed by the tiny talented trio.

Singing a capella was fun for a while, but the guys really longed to sing along with instruments.

"We wanted to make our own music instead of singing to a background track all the time," Ike explains.

So the question became, what instruments should Ike, Tay, and Zac play? All three boys played the piano, but let's face it, you don't need three pianos in a band. Taylor spoke up first and took the keyboard position. That was actually fine with Ike, because he felt the guitar would give him the new and different inspiration he'd been looking for. The only problem was, he didn't have a guitar. But in true Isaac problem-solving fashion, he picked himself up and went to the pawn store to buy one. Zac took the only instrument that was left—the drums. His first drum kit was borrowed from a neighborhood pal.

The Hanson brothers had been playing instruments together as a band for only one week when they gave their first live performance. They were so happy to be playing their own music that they didn't care that they weren't particularly good.

"Look, when you start out, you aren't as good as you are now," Ike explains, making no apologies.

But practice makes perfect, they say, and in a matter of a few short, rehearsal-filled months, the Hansons were making beautiful music together.

Adding instruments to their a capella music gave the Hanson brothers a whole new sound. And before long, they were ready to put that sound on a CD. But the recording industry had given up on pop music—calling it a dinosaur left over from the 1970s. Twelve record companies turned down the chance to work with Ike, Zac, and Tay. You can bet those record companies are sorry now. After all, for the first time ever, a dinosaur was about to come back to life—with a big *roar!*

⭐ 5

INDEPENDENTS DAY

Most bands would have given up after the first rejection, never mind the twelfth. But once Ike Hanson puts his mind to something, there's no turning back. And Ike's determination was contagious—his brothers weren't giving up, either. In 1995, the Hansons (who had finally become Hanson) went ahead and recorded their own CD, called *Boomerang!* This first Hanson independent album has been described as full of slick pop in the style of Boyz 2 Men meets Ace of Base.

Some local record stores in Tulsa took a few copies of *Boomerang* to sell. Diana Hanson took it upon herself to distribute the other copies, setting up small booths at Hanson shows to sell her sons' independent effort to local fans. Although *Boomerang* wasn't a huge hit, Ike and his brothers already had become fascinated with the recording studio. They liked being able to manipulate their voices and take the time to try different harmonies that were harder to work out onstage. At one point, Ike and Tay even ran home from the recording studio to record their voices on walkie-talkies to get a certain sound they desired.

One recorded album just couldn't fulfill Ike, Tay, and Zac's creative juices. So, before long, the brothers went back into a small Tulsa studio to record their second independent CD, *MMMBop*.

The *MMMBop* album featured everyone's favorite hit single of 1997, but the original version of "MMMBop" was much slower than the one fans recognize today. Still, it's amazing that "MMMBop" was ever recorded at all, since it was never meant to be a song.

"We started it in 1994," Isaac explains. "It was supposed to be a background part for one of the songs we were writing for *Boomerang.*"

Obviously, "MMMBop" developed a life of its own.

Ike took the recording of his early albums very seriously. He was determined to make *Boomerang* and *MMMBop* showcases for the Hanson sound. But, in typical Ike fashion, it was impossible for him not to joke around—if only just a little.

"Isaac loves to do cartoon character voices,"

recalls Louis Drapp, the owner of the production studio where *MMMBop* was recorded. "We'd be in the middle of recording, and he'd just start talking in a character voice, and everybody would just fall apart laughing."

"MMMBop" has worked mmmagic for Hanson. Not only would a remixed version of the album's title song go on to become Hanson's first worldwide number one hit, but the *MMMBop* album helped get the boys their big break.

Soon after the album was recorded, Hanson's manager, Los Angeles-based music attorney Christopher Sabec, forwarded the *MMMBop* CD to Steve Greenberg, a vice president of artists and repertoire (A&R) at Mercury records. It's Steve's job to find new acts for the label. Sure, Steve liked *MMMBop*—a lot. (Steve is obviously a man of taste!) But he wasn't looking to sign up some kiddie novelty act. And as much as he liked the musicianship he heard on the CD, Steve found it hard to believe that the songs on the CD actually had been written and recorded by three kids.

If Steve's nervousness seems odd, remember that back in 1996, it hadn't been that long since the mega-hot singing duo Milli Vanilli was exposed as a fake. (The two singers for the multi-platinum group—Rob Pilatus and Fabrice Morvan—turned out to be nothing more than lip-syncing front men who moved their mouths to prerecordings of other people's voices.) Arista

Records had really taken a bad fall on that one. So record company A&R people had learned to be extra careful.

Still, Steve couldn't get the Hanson sound out of his mind. He decided that the best way to determine whether Hanson was for real was to hear them appear live at a country fair. So Steve took off to hear them.

He signed them up the very same day.

In an "MMMBop" second, Ike and his brothers were on their way to Los Angeles to record their first major record album.

And the rest, as they say, is history!

MIDDLE OF THE STUDIO

Mercury Records had a lot of faith in Hanson, and the company was determined to make Hanson's third album a huge hit. To do that, the record company decided to put some big guns behind the recording. For starters, they hired the Dust Brothers, John King and Michael Simpson, to produce the album. The Dust Brothers are some of the hottest producers in the music business today. They were responsible for producing Beck's multiplatinum album, *Odelay*. The Dust Brothers can pick and choose what acts they want to work with, and they chose Hanson—mostly because they thought it was great that the guys played their own instruments.

But Mercury didn't stop there. They also brought in platinum-selling songwriters like Mark Hudson (who wrote "Living on the Edge" for Aerosmith), Ellen Shipley (who authored Belinda Carlisle's "Heaven is a Place on Earth"), and Barry Mann and Cynthia Weil (best known for writing "You've Lost That Loving Feeling" for the Righteous Brothers) to cowrite nine of the CD's tracks with the Hanson brothers. But you can be assured that the Hansons had the most say and the final approval on every note, lyric, and sound that appeared on the record. So the sound you hear is pure Hanson!

At first, Ike was uncomfortable with the idea of other people working on Hanson's music. After all, the boys had been responsible for all of the musical input on *Boomerang* and *MMMBop.*

"It was weird at first, just learning to work with other people and exchange ideas," he explains. "But they (the Dust Brothers) were really cool to work with. The whole vibe of the studio was very laidback. They played us different records—Three Dog Night, the Pointer Sisters, and the entire Beatles collection. It was really cool."

Most importantly, the Dust Brothers didn't try to change Hanson's sound. They simply added their own expertise. "They added some interesting elements that we might not have thought of," Ike acknowledges.

The album, which the boys decided to call *Middle of Nowhere,* took six months to record. Over the course of the recording, Mercury Records had spent a lot of money on the album's production. They weren't about to let it tank. So Mercury went ahead and gave the album a publicity blitz worthy of some of the music industry's hottest stars.

Prior to the album going on sale, Ike, Zac, and Tay appeared in *Billboard* magazine alongside two Mercury execs and the Dust Brothers. When *Billboard* runs a photo like that, it means the record label is about to kick off a huge fuss about a new album. And *huge* wasn't the word for the Hanson publicity blitz. Even before the album was released, Mercury made sure that the "MMMBop" single was all over the airwaves. And all the major record chains were made aware of the Hanson sound. Retailers and music sellers alike were already hot for Hanson when *Middle of Nowhere* was finally officially released on May 6, 1997.

In the weeks immediately following *Middle of Nowhere*'s release, Hanson headed to New York City for a series of TV and magazine interviews which included stints on the *Rosie O'Donnell Show, Live with Regis and Kathie Lee, MTV News,* and *The Late Show with David Letterman.* But the biggest Hanson news didn't take place in New York—it took place in Oklahoma. The exact same day that Hanson was in New York doing *Letterman,* the governor of Oklahoma was busy declaring May 6 to be Hanson Day in the boys' home state.

The boys' hugest concert to date was at the Paramus Park mall in a New Jersey suburb not far from New York City. The concert came only one day after *Middle of Nowhere* went on sale, but already the mall was packed. The boys had no idea how loved they had become. When the Hansons' limo pulled into the mall's packed parking lot, Ike thought all the cars were there because Sears was having a sale! But there wasn't any sale. All those people were there to welcome Hanson to New Jersey and to the world of stardom.

After the New York area promo tour, Ike and his brothers jetted back to Los Angeles for a spot on the *Tonight* show with Jay Leno and a promotional concert at a local Sam Goody's, which attracted hundreds of screaming fans. The fans had begun lining up at nine A.M. to hear Hanson—even though the boys weren't scheduled to perform until one.

Phew! What a week! And the work didn't stop there. As soon as they finished taping with Leno, the boys took a limo back to the airport and headed for another stop in New York, which included a stint on the nation's number one morning show, the *Today* show.

After all that, the boys definitely had earned a few days off—and they took their R&R in the Big Apple, sightseeing at the Statue of Liberty, the World Trade Center, and other popular tourist attractions. They hardly realized that they had already become tourist attractions themselves!

But the well-deserved rest didn't last long. Before long, the Hansons were back on a plane and headed for Europe. (Rumor has it they traveled coach, just to prove how little they'd changed.) Promoting *Middle of Nowhere* had become a full-time job.

But all the hard work eventually paid off. By the end of the summer of 1997, "MMMBop" was an international sensation, hitting the number one spot in Australia, Austria, Argentina, Belgium, Canada, England, Denmark, Finland, Germany, Hungary, Indonesia, Ireland, Sweden, Israel, Japan, the Netherlands, New Zealand, Switzerland, and the United States. One reviewer suggested that a reason for the song's international success was that the tune's catchy chorus means the same in any language.

Having a hit single is something Isaac Hanson had barely allowed himself to dream of. Having the number one single in the world was beyond all his dreams.

But "MMMBop" was just the beginning. The successful release of Hanson's second single from *Middle of Nowhere,* "Where's the Love," and the third single, "I Will Come to You," proved that Hanson was no one-hit wonder. And if skeptics felt that Hanson had only one great album in them, the November 1997 release of

Snowed In, the boys' top-ten Christmas album, proved them wrong.

Instead of dying down, Hansonmania appears to be just gearing up. There's no limit to the success Ike and his brothers can achieve. They are sure to go from the middle of nowhere to the top of the world!

7

TULSA, TOKYO, AND THE MIDDLE OF NOWHERE

England, France, Germany, Korea, Japan, Australia! The summer and fall of 1997 were a whirlwind around-the-world adventure for Ike, Tay, and Zac. Touring the world and giving interviews to radio, TV, and magazine reporters were really special experiences for the brothers H. And, in keeping with their total devotion to their fans, Ike and his bros decided to tape the whole tour and share the fun with the people who have made them the success they are. The final result of this awesome video project, *Tulsa, Tokyo, and the Middle of Nowhere,* is Hanson's hot new long-format video. It was released last November.

Much of *Tulsa, Tokyo, and the Middle of Nowhere* was filmed during Hanson's huge worldwide two-month press tour, and it gives viewers a never-before-seen look at what it's like to travel with Ike (and Tay and Zac, of course). The tape gets so up-close and personal that for eighty-two minutes (that's how long the video runs), you really feel as though you're on the road *with* Hanson!

Some of the most interesting footage is the backstage shots of Hanson before they go on-stage. It's kind of incredible to see the crowd at New Jersey's Paramus Park mall through Isaac, Tay, and Zac's eyes. From their point of view, the whole mall was a sea of hands, legs, and screaming people—all wanting a piece of Hanson. (And some of the girls got exactly that—Ike is quick to point out that one of the screaming girls ripped off a piece of Tay's shirt!)

In fact, it seems that everywhere the boys went during their world publicity tour, the fans turned out in huge numbers. The guys always loved meeting up with their fans, even if it was a little weird at times. For instance, there was one really bizarre radio interview in Japan. The radio station was at the very end of a mall. The station was all enclosed in glass, and fans paraded by the glass walls in lines, hoping for a glimpse of their favorite Hanson. The boys all agreed that it was a little difficult trying to focus on answering questions while waving to their fans at the same time.

Of course, the first word in the video's title is *Tulsa,* and some of the most intimate scenes in the video are shot right in the boys' hometown. If you've ever wondered what the famous Hanson garage looks like (that's the place where Ike, Tay, and Zac come up with so many of their tunes), *Tulsa, Tokyo, and the Middle of Nowhere* is the place for you.

The video is filled with home movies shot at the Hanson home in Tulsa. Many of those home movies are extra-cool because they were shot with Ike's new video camera. Ike's become quite the cameraman, and he hardly goes anywhere without his camcorder. (He once shot footage of Taylor sleeping—shots that even the biggest Hanson fan would probably find a little boring!) You can spot Ike's footage in *Tulsa, Tokyo, and the Middle of Nowhere* right away—they say "Ikecam" in the corner of the screen. Ike's footage is a true Hanson-eye view of Ike, Tay, and Zac's daily lives. (And, by the way, Ike's not the only cameraman in the Hanson clan. Check out the credits at the end of the video, and you'll discover that Hanson dad Walker shot a great deal of the video footage.)

It is during one of those wacky home-video scenes that Ike's fans really get to see the unbelievably goofy side of Hanson's guitar guru. The guys got together and made a fake documentary video about redwood trees. They called the video documentary "Mild Kingdom," which, of course, is a take-off on the old TV nature show *Wild Kingdom.* In the fake documentary, Ike mugs for the camera and speaks in all sorts of wacko accents, calling himself Joe, Doctor of Treeology. Zac really gets into the fake documentary, too, pretending to be a reporter who is interviewing Ike. Only Tay manages to stay out of the fray; he doesn't seem to want to have anything to do with his brothers' wacky escapades.

As if all that weren't enough, *Tulsa, Tokyo, and the Middle of Nowhere* has an added bonus for Hanson fans—a fresh new edit of the "Where's the Love" video. Isaac is quick to tell his fans that they will definitely "see things you never saw before."

Tulsa, Tokyo, and the Middle of Nowhere is peppered with tons of really cool interviews with the brothers H. It's the best way ever for fans to get inside those handsome Hanson heads and find out just how it feels to be a member of one of the top bands in the world.

And if you've ever wondered what it's like to be in the studio with Hanson, here's your chance to find out. There's plenty of footage of the guys recording—and yelling at one another for coming in late with the notes. Still, in the end, the guys make beautiful music together. (Dontcha just love a happy ending?)

Tulsa, Tokyo, and the Middle of Nowhere opens and closes with scenes from a single concert, filmed at New York's famous Beacon Theater. Playing the Beacon is further proof of just how far Hanson has come from the old days when they jammed at high school auditoriums. The Beacon is a grand old theater that has played host to some really huge names in rap, pop, jazz, gospel, and classical music. But if those plush velvet curtains that line the stage could talk, they would surely say that no one who has played the Beacon has ever had a reception like Hanson's.

The crowd was so rowdy that the Beacon management had to lay down a few ground rules. First they told everyone not to take flash photos of Hanson. Then they reminded the crowd not to stand on the seats. From the looks of the video, no one was listening.

Ike, Taylor, and Zac had their own set of rules for the crowd. Their only rule was that no one was allowed to stand still. After all, a Hanson concert is a lot like a big party—and when you party, you gotta dance!

Hanson's rule ruled. From the very minute Tay shouted out, "Are you ready to rock?" the crowd got onto its feet and sang along with six hits from *Middle of Nowhere*.

But it was Ike who gave the audience its biggest thrill of the night. He bent down and gave the lucky fans in the front row a close-up view of the fancy fingerwork on his guitar licks. All those years of live performances have really paid off. Ike truly knows how to work a crowd! And watching Ike's face, you can see that making the audience happy is his ultimate thrill.

"It's just so fun for us," Ike says of performing

live. "It's just so cool that all these people are having fun, and dancing and clapping to your music."

But don't be fooled into thinking that the Beacon show was a normal Hanson concert. For starters, fans couldn't buy tickets for the Hanson show. They had to win them from New York radio station Z-100. And since the concert was being taped for the video, the guys had to run through the show twice—something no one in the audience seemed to mind. After all, that meant the audience members were twice as lucky!

If you weren't fortunate enough to see the show, don't feel bad. Thanks to the magic of video, you can see Ike and bros up-close and personal—right in your own living room!

8

FIFTY-FIVE FACTS AT YOUR FINGERTIPS!

1. Ike is five feet ten inches tall—for now. He may still be growing.
2. Ike's eyes are light brown.
3. *Middle of Nowhere* was Hanson's third album. The first two, *Boomerang* and *MMMBop!*, were self-produced independent albums.
4. It was Ike's idea to take the cab and the bus you see in the "MMMBop" video.
5. Before Mercury signed Hanson to a record deal, the brothers had written almost two hundred songs.
6. Ike doesn't have a girlfriend right now.
7. Ike loves being home-schooled.
8. Ike's favorite sports are Rollerblading and street hockey.
9. The Hanson brothers wrote "Thinking of You" in less than half an hour.

10. Ike keeps his body toned. His average weight is a slim 135 pounds.
11. Ike's favorite color is green.
12. Isaac's favorite kind of book is science fiction.
13. Ike's favorite movie is *Star Wars.*
14. Tay's nickname for Ike is "Chewbacca."
15. Zac's nicknames for Ike are "Braceface" and "Ikey-poo."
16. Ike likes chunky peanut butter better than creamy.
17. The scar on Tay's face is partially Isaac's fault. Ike was chasing Tay, and Tay wasn't watching where he was going. Tay slammed into a door, and the rest is history.
18. Ike's favorite classic rocker is Chuck Berry.
19. Ike's favorite ice cream flavor is vanilla.
20. Isaac isn't big on accessories the way his brother Tay is. His only jewelry is a single silver ring (which he wears on the middle finger of his left hand) and his watch.
21. Ike's favorite item of clothing is his old brown leather jacket.
22. Isaac and his brothers have become so famous that they have to travel with bodyguards everywhere they go.
23. Before he grew up to write songs about relationships, friendships, and other meaningful topics, Ike penned odes to little-boy love objects like frogs and ants.

24. Ike's idea of a dream dinner is pasta, lasagna, and steak—all at once!
25. Ike's favorite fast food is pizza.
26. Ike's never been a big tennis player, but ever since Hanson's performance at Arthur Ashe Kids Day in New York, he's decided to take up the sport.
27. Ike is known as the romantic member of the band.
28. Ike is a junior in high school.
29. Ike's dream car is a Corvette—then again, whose isn't?
30. Ike is considered the most businesslike member of the group.
31. Ike's favorite actors are Mel Gibson, Arnold Schwarzenegger, and Harrison Ford.
32. Ike, Tay, and Zac modeled their early harmonies on those of the Beach Boys.
33. The brothers H are working on painting a huge mural on the wall of their garage music room.
34. Ike drinks diet soda.
35. Isaac's braces are clear plastic.
36. Ike, Tay, and Zac once did twenty-one interviews in a single day.
37. Ike once had his hair cut really, really short—and he says he may do it again someday. (Say it ain't so, Ike!)
38. Isaac has said that if he could take any one thing to the moon with him, it would be his

little cousin Wayne because he's so sweet. (All together now . . . *awwww!)*

39. Ike's dream girl is Cindy Crawford—whom he actually got to visit one afternoon. Their meeting can be seen on the *Tulsa, Tokyo, and the Middle of Nowhere* video.

40. The Hanson brothers have a halfpipe skating ramp in their Tulsa backyard.

41. The brothers designed the Hanson logo themselves.

42. Ike likes to shop at the Gap. He also likes Old Navy jeans.

43. Ike likes to relax by playing table tennis (or Ping-Pong).

44. Although Isaac is known for his guitar work, he's also a classically trained pianist.

45. Many people think Ike looks like actor Stephen Baldwin.

46. Ike carries a journal with him wherever he goes.

47. Reviewers refer to Ike as "the serious one" of the group.

48. Ike once told Tay to blow his nose—on national television!

49. Ike has a pet turtle he brings with him on tour when he can.

50. When the guys were in London, they got in trouble for Rollerblading in the hall of a five-star hotel.

51. Someday, Ike would like to produce albums for other groups besides Hanson.

52. The "MMMBop" video was taped in Malibu and Hollywood, California.
53. Ike is the only Hanson brother with a driver's license.
54. Ike got his first guitar at a pawn shop.
55. Ike once got in trouble for holding a girl's hand at the circus.

CLARKE

HANSON

ISAAC

(Ernie Paniccioli/Retna)

(Ernest Paniccioli/Shooting Star)

(Steve Granitz/Retna)

(Ernie Paniccioli/Retna)

(Celebrity Photo Agency)

(Ernie Paniccioli/Retna)

'ROUND AND 'ROUND

9

SON NUMBER ONE

It's a heavy responsibility being the eldest brother when Hanson goes on tour. Although the boys' parents are usually with them, Ike feels real pressure to take care of his two younger brothers. "He's the one who always makes sure we all have our pitch pipes," Tay jokes.

Ike's genuine desire to take care of his brothers may be a result of the fact that he is the first of Walker and Diana's children. Many scientists believe that a portion of people's personalities is formed because of the order in which they were born in their families. Ike definitely has a lot of the characteristics that scientists have indentified in a firstborn child.

As the eldest, Isaac Hanson heavily identifies with his parents. In fact, he has said that part of the reason he chose the guitar as his instrument in the band was that he wanted to follow in his father's footsteps. Ike is the first to defend his folks to the press. Whenever anyone accuses Walker and Diana of pushing their kids too hard, it is Ike who quickly explains that the guys haven't been pushed into showbiz by two star-struck parents. "They'd support us in anything we wanted to do. They've just been there to back us up," he told a reporter from the Reuters news service.

Ike has learned a lot from his caring parents, and he's used that knowledge to help his brothers out when they are away from home. Ike, like many firstborns, sometimes puts himself in the surrogate-parent position—especially when it comes to keeping an eye on wildman Hanson brother Zac. But Ike doesn't boss his little bro around. Instead, he tries to treat him with respect, which naturally makes Zac want to temper his wacky moods to meet Ike's high expectations.

Ike also will go to great lengths to protect his brothers—even when it means putting himself in danger. Take the time he was forced to defend Taylor in a fight.

"I got into a fight once because a guy picked on Tay," Isaac says. "He was a good friend, and he threw Taylor against a wall and made his nose bleed. I went really mad. He wasn't a good friend after that."

Ike's sense of responsibility isn't limited to keeping his bros in line in the hotel room. He makes sure they tow the line in the studio, too. If the brothers have an argument, it's Ike who tells Tay and Zac to snap out of it. Ike knows there's no room for fussing and pouting in the studio. No matter how angry his brothers may be, "you still gotta rehearse," he says wisely.

Many of the adults who helped Hanson produce *Middle of Nowhere* were incredibly impressed with Ike's sense of brotherly responsibility in the studio. "He really looks out for the little ones," explains Mark Hudson, the songwriter who coproduced Hanson's Christmas '97 album, *Snowed In.* And Mark doesn't just mean that Ike looks out for Tay and Zac. Ike looks out for the littlest Hansons—Jessica, Avery, and Mackenzie—too. Ike feels it is extremely important that they be protected from the press (which is part of the reason you rarely see any pix of the three younger sibs) and that they feel no pressure to perform like their older brothers.

"It's important that (Jessica, Avery, and Mackenzie) feel free to do what they want," he says when asked if his youngest sibs will someday join Hanson or start a group all their own.

Ike is incredibly tolerant of Tay and Zac's antics. Even though he has a lot to say about Hanson and the music they make, his speeches inevitably get interrupted by Tay and Zac. But Ike takes this in his stride. He's just glad to be working with his best friends, who just happen to be his brothers.

Most importantly, Ike feels good knowing that he's there for his brothers and that, in return, they're there for him. After all, the Hanson brothers are experiencing a lifestyle that few people will ever know. In fact, the only people who will ever completely understand what they've been going through are Ike, Tay, and Zac. And brotherly support is really important when you're being followed by huge mobs of shrieking fans. "It can be a bit scary when twenty or thirty people are running at your car," Ike explains.

Ike also feels a commitment to kids everywhere. In fact, one of his ambitions is to be a music teacher someday, so he can spread his love of music to kids all over the world.

Like a lot of firstborns, Ike has acted like a grown-up for almost his whole life. As Tay puts it, "He was the kind of guy who knew he was going to get married in the third grade."

But that doesn't mean that Ike can't be silly. Take last November 22, when Hanson hosted SNICK, Nickelodeon's Saturday night programs. Ike joined right in with his brothers in promotional spots for the "Cooking with Hanson" comedy routine, gleefully pouring orange soda into a large bowl filled with peanut butter, marshmallow, and cereal. *(Blech!)*

Stay away from the kitchen, and stick to the music, okay, Ike?

THE SENSITIVE SCORPIO

Ike's birthday is November 17, which makes him a Scorpio. Like any Scorpio, Ike is incredibly passionate about everything he does, whether it's writing music, appearing in a video, or dating that special girl. And that passion is often visible in his writing—and we don't mean just his song lyrics. Ike has been known to write some pretty intense letters to the ladies in his life.

"I like writing letters," Ike replied when he was asked how romantic he was. "Taylor once threw a letter I'd written to a girl into a fountain because he thought it was disgusting."

Most guys would be too embarrassed to write a love letter, never mind having their innermost feelings recorded in songs that are heard by millions of people. But none of that bothers Ike.

Scorpios are known for their confidence, and Ike is no exception.

Scorpios stick to their beliefs. Ike can hold his ground with anyone. Take the Hanson photo sessions in New York's Central Park. The photographers wanted Hanson to be photographed with cute stuffed animals—an adorable shot, no doubt, but certainly not in keeping with Hanson's image. The last thing the guys want to do is remind people of how young they are. The photographers argued that the photo would make the ultimate pinup for fans' walls. But Ike stood his ground and refused. In the end, Ike won out.

It just goes to show that Scorpios can't be forced to change their opinions—not for all the money in the world. Of course, that's because money doesn't mean much to Scorpios.

"Money is only the icing on the cake," Ike told *Superteen* magazine. "If you're successful and you get to make a living off what you love to do, then why not go for it? If you make pottery and you can make money selling it to people, then why not do it? If we didn't make a single cent off of what we're doing, we would still perform, because that's what we intend to do for the rest of our lives."

And that's cool with your fans, Ike, because they intend to be listening to Hanson's music for the rest of *their* lives.

MONKEYIN' AROUND
WITH IKE

Once, when he was fifteen years old, Ike sprained his ankle pretty badly. "I was climbing a plum tree and just fell out and tried to land on my feet. My ankle gave way and swelled up," he explains. "The doctors thought I had broken it, but it was just really badly bruised."

What was Ike doing up in that tree, swinging around like a monkey? He says he's not really sure. Maybe he really *is* a monkey—or, at least, he was born under the sign of the Monkey, according to Chinese astrology.

The theory behind the Chinese zodiac is that your birth year can influence how you act and even foretell what kind of career you might try in the future. Each birth year in the Chinese zodiac is named for a particular animal. The people born under that sign supposedly take on some of the characteristics of that animal.

People born under the sign of the Monkey are fun-loving and usually very cheerful. Monkeys are also extremely creative and clever—they can turn even the most boring story into a fanciful tale that captures an audience's imagination. In Ike's case, he writes lyrics that tell stories that capture his fans' hearts.

Invite a person born under the sign of the Monkey to a party (and who wouldn't want to invite Ike to their party?), and the Monkey will become the center of attention as soon as he walks in the door. The key to a Monkey's charm and popularity is his humor. And Ike's wacky sense of humor is certainly a big aspect of his personality!

One thing's for sure, Ike had better never play cards for money. It is nearly impossible for a Monkey to develop a poker face. People born under the sign of the Monkey find it extremely difficult to hide their emotions. They want everyone to know how happy—or depressed—they are. Of course, it is this ability to be in touch with his feelings that allows Ike to write such beautiful and meaningful music and lyrics. Although the Hansons write all of their songs as a team, it is often Ike who will suggest writing the beautiful ballads his fans so adore.

People born under the sign of the Monkey are good listeners. They are also very good at working out solutions to their friends' problems. If you're totally bummed out one day, just dial a Monkey! Wouldn't it be great if you really could just dial Ike's number on the phone and talk to him when you really need him? Of course, you can't, but listening to his music is guaranteed to get you through even the saddest days.

People born under the sign of the Monkey have a real thirst for knowledge, which may explain why Ike considers his home-schooling an incredibly positive experience. While they were in London, Ike and his brothers studied British history while touring the dungeons and the Tower of London. "We're always experiencing new people and new cultures," Ike explained to the British press. "How many U.S. history teachers would die to be able to send their classes to London?"

As a person born under the inquisitive, creative sign of the Monkey, Ike has a thirst for knowledge that allows him to explore avenues beyond his music. For the past two years, he's been writing a science-fiction novel. He's had to study the real science behind his plot line. And science has become one of his favorite subjects.

Science has become one of Ike's fans' favorite subjects as well. Most of them are into zoology— with a heavy concentration on the study of a really hunky monkey named Clarke Isaac Hanson!

ARE YOU IKE'S TYPE?

Ike Hanson has often described himself as technical, artsy, and romantic. Well, his brothers don't necessarily have any comment on the technical or artsy stuff, but they do have plenty to say about Ike's romantic prowess.

"Ike is a girl charmer," Zac confides. "He'll always say nice things to girls. It's just a thing he does."

"Ike thinks about girls all the time," Tay agrees.

And Ike is characteristically quiet on the subject of the ladies in his life. "We don't want to get into the whole dating thing. It's about the music," he's been known to tell nosy reporters who ask too many questions about his love life. And the truth is, Ike hasn't really had that much time to get into the whole dating thing himself—he spends most of his time doing interviews and performing.

The girl for Ike has to be very special. For starters, she'd have to be tolerant of Ike's busy schedule. And she'd have to be secure enough to know that although Ike is surrounded by screaming girls all the time, she's still the special one. A jealous girl probably could never emotionally handle the huge crowd of Hanson fans that would always be blowing kisses to her guy. There would be consolation for her, however. All three Hansons say that they will sign autographs, shake hands, and take pictures with their fans, but they are saving their kisses for someone special someday.

And as with everything else in his life, Ike has a positive attitude about finding that special someone. "We'll definitely have girlfriends in the future," he says, "but that will have to work itself out."

Ike is clearly optimistic: "None of us has a girlfriend right now, but you meet people everywhere you go, and I know mine will turn up someday."

Ike's not a kiss-and-tell kind of guy. But he does tend to name his guitars after girls he likes, and two of his guitars have been named Hannah and Keisha. Who are Hannah and Keisha? Only Ike knows for sure. The important thing is that Ike's new guitar is currently nameless—and that means there's a spot for one lucky girl in Ike's heart.

If *you* should ever be lucky enough to go out on a date with Ike one day, what can you expect? Well, for starters, make sure you have permission to go on a car date, because Isaac has his license now, and he loves driving! Ike may take you to a movie, but don't look forward to cuddling up in his arms and watching a sweet, romantic film. Tear-jerker movies just aren't Isaac's kind of thing.

"I can't remember the last time I cried," he says. "I must have been really young. I've never cried at a movie or a TV show. I'm just not a guy who cries easily."

Ike's taste in flicks tends more toward the action-adventure side. And if you think about it, that can actually be kind of cool—especially if you need to hold on to him during the scary parts!

After the movie, Isaac just might take you out for a huge pizza—it's his favorite junk food. Going out for a snack can also give you a chance to talk and get to know each other—something Ike feels is absolutely necessary before he can make a commitment to someone. But beware—Ike's a real clown. He's liable to make a bunch of silly faces or talk in wild accents just to make you laugh. Try not to laugh too hard—your soda might come out your nose. And, boy, could that be a turnoff.

When he's not goofing around, Ike loves to talk about his music (natch!), but he's also interested in other people's music. And you might want to read up on a few good sci-fi books before your big date. And whatever you do, don't start comparing Hanson to other famous pop groups. Ike doesn't like it when people start comparing his music to others'. He feels strongly that Hanson's music is unique—and he's right!

If you're lucky, after the pizza, Ike may take you to a video arcade to show off his prowess with the latest machines. Arcades give Ike a chance to show off his techno-genius side. He's a whiz with the games!

One thing's for sure, Ike won't be wishy-washy about what you two will do on your dream date. He's got strong ideas about things. Luckily, he's also willing to compromise and consider other people's feelings. Besides, as far as Ike is concerned, it doesn't matter what you do on a date. "As long as you're on a date with someone you really like, it doesn't matter where you are or what you do," he declares.

That's true. The only ingredients needed for a perfect date are Isaac Hanson and you!

IKE'S RECORD COLLECTION

When Isaac sits down to listen to some music, it isn't Hanson albums he puts on his stereo. Ike's too critical of each and every note to make listening to himself much of a pleasant experience. Ike's more likely to put on other people's music. And Ike's tastes really run the gamut, from early rock and rhythm-and-blues to alternative music to country. So no matter which section you may be checking out in your local record store, you could run into Ike Hanson!

You can hear the influence of many musical greats in every song on *Middle of Nowhere*. For instance, there's the gospel-tinged rock tune "I Will Come to You," the Jackson Five-esque "Where Is the Love," and the Beatles-influenced ballad "Lucy."

If you really want to get into Ike's head (and who wouldn't? he's one interesting, smart guy), you'll have to listen to some of the same music he does. Check out a few tunes or albums by these cool musical artists. They're some of Ike's faves.

SPIN DOCTORS

Ike has often said that if he had a spare twenty dollars, he'd buy a Spin Doctors CD. It's no wonder. People who have analyzed the Spin Doctors sound have remarked that the group found its influences in the same 1960s sounds as Hanson has. And, like Hanson, Spin Doctors singer Chris Barron acknowledges the influences but says he's built on them. "Sure, similarities exist," Chris says of the Spin Doctors' relationship with the music of the past. "After all, rock-and-roll feeds on its past. But it's lazy to say that's all we are." Now, there's a philosophy Ike can relate to. He gets equally upset when people write off Hanson's music as 1990s Jackson Five.

Besides 1960s R&B, Spin Doctors has been heavily influenced by the lyrics of rock-and-roll legend Bob Dylan. And that's another reason Spin Doctors is one of Ike's favorite bands. Isaac has often said that literature and history are two of his favorite subjects in school. Words and the meanings behind them are extremely important to Ike.

To check out some vintage Spin Doctors, get your hands on a copy of *Pocket Full of Kryptonite.*

COUNTING CROWS

Singer and pianist Adam Duritz joined guitarist David Bryson to form Counting Crows back in 1991 in San Francisco. By the time Geffen Records signed them to a record contract, they'd already added guitarist Dan Vickrey, bassist Matt Malley, and drummer Steve Bowman to the band's roster. Ben Mize later replaced Steve Bowman on drums.

It's no surprise that someone who has as much knowledge of rock-and-roll history as Ike does would love Counting Crows. The group has its roots in a lot of the same rock sources as Hanson does. In fact, *Melody Maker* magazine once described Counting Crows as a band "unashamedly steeped in the classic rock tradition, but there's nothing stale . . . about their music." Check out *August and Everything After,* the band's debut album.

ALANIS MORISSETTE

It's kind of "ironic" that Ike Hanson enjoys the music of Alanis Morissette. The two musicians have a whole lot in common. The twenty-three-year-old singer, who is best known for her multiplatinum album *Jagged Little Pill,* actually was a child prodigy who started taking piano lessons at age six. By age eleven, Alanis had released her first single, "Fate Stay with Me." And by the time she was twelve, she was starring in a Canadian TV show called *You Can't Do That on Television.* So if anyone could understand what Ike has been going through the past year or so, it would be Alanis. You can get an idea of the thoughts going on in Alanis's head by picking up a copy of her four-time Grammy award-winning album, *Jagged Little Pill.*

NO DOUBT

Hanson's music may be upbeat and pop-oriented, but that doesn't mean that Ike can't appreciate a great new wave band. And he does. Ike's fave of this genre is No Doubt, a totally awesome new wave/ska band headed by lead singer Gwen Stefani. The band started out as just Gwen and her brother Eric. But by the time No Doubt hit the big time, Eric had left to become an animator on *The Simpsons.* (That's kind of ironic, too, since Ike and his brothers have often thought about animating their own characters in some of their videos.) If you want to check out No Doubt's sound—and no doubt you will— pick up their chart-topping album *Tragic Kingdom.*

GARTH BROOKS

It might surprise you to know that Hanson is only the *second* most successful musical act to come from Tulsa. The honor of the number one spot goes to country music's current reigning king, Garth Brooks. Garth's sold 62 million albums to date, making him the best-selling solo artist of all time (he's sold even more albums than the King of Rock and Roll, Elvis Presley). Garth's very first album, *Garth Brooks,* was the best-selling country album of the entire 1980s. So, if you want to hear genuine Oklahoma country sounds, be sure to check out these Garth Brooks classics: *Garth Brooks, Ropin' the Wind,* and *The Chase.*

CHUCK BERRY

Chuck Berry has influenced more of rock's legends than just about any other pioneer of rock-and-roll. Chuck Berry's hits of the 1950s were some of the first to catch the fancy of John Lennon and Paul McCartney. They later recorded many of his songs with a little band they played in. (Perhaps you've heard of that band—they were called the Beatles.) Mick Jagger and Keith Richards also list Chuck as one of their early idols, and the Rolling Stones recorded their share of Chuck's tunes, too. Now Chuck Berry can add Isaac Hanson to his long list of incredibly famous and talented fans. If you're looking for some familiar Chuck Berry songs to rock with, check out these litle ditties: "Roll Over Beethoven," "Johnny B. Goode," "Sweet Little Sixteen," and "Come On."

THE BEATLES

Ever since Hanson burst onto the scene, people have been comparing them to the Beatles. But as far as Ike is concerned, Hanson's music is unique. If you mention the comparison, Ike is sure to cut you short with a simple "Don't go there, okay?"

Although the Beatles' music is thirty years old, it still sounds pretty incredible today. That may explain why Ike is so into the band. Check out these awesome Beatles albums: *Meet the Beatles, Rubber Soul, Sgt. Pepper's Lonely Hearts Club Band* and *Abbey Road*.

BILLY JOEL

Isaac Hanson was raised on the music of Billy Joel, much the same way other kids were raised on lullabies. One of the first songs Ike, Tay, and Zac ever harmonized on was Billy's "For the Longest Time." But, like Hanson and the Beatles, Billy Joel writes and records songs in a myriad of styles—pop, rock, R&B. To check out the many sounds of Billy Joel, take a listen to these albums: *Piano Man, The Stranger, Kohuept* (a live concert from the former Soviet Union), and *The Nylon Curtain*.

CHRIS STAMEY AND THE DBS ("Christmas Time"), ***THE BEACH BOYS*** ("Little Saint Nick"), ***OTIS REDDING*** ("White Christmas"). Okay, you caught us. These are all the artists who originally recorded songs that appear on Hanson's newest album, *Snowed In*. More than any other Hanson album, *Snowed In* shows just how much Isaac and his brothers have been influenced by other artists, since all but four of the songs on the album were written and originally performed by people other than Hanson. As the boys said in the liner notes, "We love the celebration of Christmas and also the songs that have become a part of our rich Christmas memories."

Here's a list of all the classic Christmas tunes on *Snowed In* that are *not* by Ike, Zac, and Tay: "Merry Christmas Baby," "What Christmas Means to Me," "Little Saint Nick," "Christmas (Baby Please Come Home)," "Rockin' Around the Christmas Tree," "Run Rudolph Run," "Silent Night Medley," and "White Christmas".

YOU'VE GOT IKE'S NUMBER!

Ike Hanson is truly number one. And not just in songwriting, guitar playing, or all-around cuteness. Ike is really a number one when it comes to numerology.

Numerology is a science that can be traced all the way back to the time of the ancient Babylonians. According to numerology, each person's personality falls into one of nine basic types. You can find out what type your favorite star (which would be Ike, of course) fits into by counting up the letters in his or her name.

Here's how we figured out that Ike was a one: First, we wrote out all of the letters in his full name (nicknames won't give you a true numerological reading), and then we matched the letters with numbers according to the following chart.

1	2	3	4	5	6	7	8	9
A	B	C	D	E	F	G	H	I
J	K	L	M	N	O	P	Q	R
S	T	U	V	W	X	Y	Z	

CLARKE ISAAC HANSON
3 3 1 9 2 5 9 1 1 1 3 8 1 5 1 6 5

We added all of the numbers in Ike's name together and got a sum of 64.

But we weren't finished yet. We added the 6 and the 4 (in 64) to get the number 10. And Ike *is* a perfect 10. But the numbers on the numerology scale only go from 1 to 9, so we added up the 1 and the 0 (in 10) and came up with a sum of 1.

To find out what ones like Ike are like, check the chart below. Then take the time to figure out your number and see what it says about you. Who knows, your number may be just the one Ike's looking for!

According to numerology, **ones** are natural-born leaders. And Ike certainly is a leader. It's Ike who keeps his brothers working toward their common goal and who makes sure cooler heads prevail when there's an argument. Ones are extremely well organized and tend to like to do all of the work themselves. Ones love the spotlight! But they also can get a reputation for being ruthless, so they have to learn to give up the limelight once in a while and share the glory.

Ones get along well with twos and sixes.

Twos are quiet and reserved. They are also very diplomatic and tend to try hard to understand both sides of a situation. But twos also can be super-sensitive. Criticism makes them brood over hurt feelings. Twos need to learn to stand up for themselves a bit more often.

Twos make good matches for sevens, eights, and other twos.

Threes are dynamic, and people are naturally drawn to them. Threes are often leaders. If threes don't learn good leadership skills, they can be in real danger of becoming very bossy, because they like having things done their way. Threes are a lot of fun to be around, but they have sharp tongues, which can sting.

Threes get along especially well with fours and fives.

Fours take duty and responsibility very seriously. They can be witty and entertaining. They are incredibly loyal pals. But watch out if a four disagrees with you—they have a tendency to speak their minds, regardless of the hurt feelings they may cause.

Fours get along very well with twos, threes,

and eights, but they really go for fives and sixes (which can be a dangerous combination!).

Your average **fives** (actually, the truth is there's nothing *average* about a five) like action, adventure, and plenty of excitement. They are smooth talkers who have no problem getting their thoughts across. But fives need to watch their wallets; they tend to let money slip right through their fingers.

Fives get along well with threes, sevens, and twos.

It's hard not to like **sixes** because they are so kind, even-tempered, and eager to help. Sixes always look for the good in people and situations. Unfortunately, sixes sometimes can be a little *too* trusting, which makes them easy marks for people who want to take advantage of them.

If you're a six, spend some time hanging out with ones, eights, and nines.

Sevens are trendsetters! They are the ones who discover the hot new song first (betcha it was a seven who first brought "MMMBop" to your attention!) or put together the outfits that the whole school winds up copying. But sevens are concerned with more than just tapes and clothes. They also can be deep thinkers who love to delve into a subject.

Sevens get along really well with nines, fours, other sevens, and eights.

Eights are incredibly self-disciplined people, with high powers of concentration. If they aim high, they almost always reach the top. Eights make great friends because they never forget a kindness. On the other hand, they never forget an injustice, either, so watch how you treat an eight.

Good matches for eights are twos, fours, sixes, sevens, and nines.

Nines are very concerned with the needs of people who have far less than they. They are the first ones to jump up and volunteer in the name of a cause—and they have little tolerance for those who don't choose to lend a hand. But sometimes that can mean trouble, because the needs of their close friends and family can take a backseat to their concern for humanity's big picture. Nines are likely to use their money and their seemingly endless stamina to help the world. But when it comes to a nine's own feelings, he or she is extremely mercurial—up one minute and down the next!

Fours, sevens, and eights make great matches for nines.

15

PSYCHIC PREDICTIONS

What does the future hold for Ike and his brothers? By the end of 1997, Hanson finally seemed destined for lasting stardom.

Snowed In was released to hit reviews, with *Music Week in the UK* saying that "these . . . tracks will ensure that the brothers enjoy annual immortality at office parties. Their rock-and-roll covers and their own new tracks make this an essential purchase." *Entertainment Weekly* chimed in with its own A− review, saying, "Those Hanson lads (have) cooked up a collection that'll not only satisfy their contemporaries but even grab grown-ups who remember the days when Brian Wilson, Phil Spector, and Otis Redding got something extra in their stockings for their efforts."

But *Snowed In* wasn't the only big news of

winter '97. Ike and his brothers finally saw the results of their whirlwind European tour when Hanson won the Best Breakthrough Act and Best Song ("MMMBop") awards at the Europe Music Awards.

So how does Hanson top 1997? For starters, Ike and his bros are definitely hoping for a big concert tour in 1998. And that makes Ike incredibly happy. Although Isaac is very comfortable in the recording studio—all those knobs and buttons are fascinating to his techno side—it's performing in front of his fans that gives Ike the biggest thrill. He says he never tires of hearing their cheers and screams. And it's a huge kick to hear the fans sing lyrics that he and his brothers have written. (Ike must have been in heaven last December 9, when a sold-out crowd at New York's Madison Square Garden sang along with "MMMBop" at a local radio station's Christmas concert in which Hanson was part of a huge celebrity lineup including Celine Dion, Aerosmith, and the Backstreet Boys.)

But let's face it, the Hansons haven't yet recorded enough tunes to carry a whole concert by themselves—even though they have written hundreds of songs together. So, the brothers are going to get a chance to sing some of their favorite '50s and '60s R&B tunes in concert. "That kind of music is very dear to us, because we've always considered it particularly inspirational," Ike explains.

There's no doubt in anyone's mind that Hanson concerts will be sell-out shows no matter where they go, which is awesome for Hanson but not so great for the fans that can't get tickets. But relax, if you become one of the unlucky ones who can't scoop up some seats to see Hanson in person, you will more than likely be able to see them up-close and personal with all of the TV appearances the boys are making these days. Ike and his brothers already have hosted Nickelodeon's SNICK Saturday night lineup and ABC's TGIF Friday night lineup.

Then, of course, there was also the awesome ABC *Meet Hanson* special last Thanksgiving weekend that brought in humongous ratings (and helped the boys promote *Snowed In* for the holiday season). In the special, veteran (but never aging) *American Bandstand* star and rock-and-roll expert Dick Clark interviewed the tasty trio about fame and music. The guys also managed to squeeze in "MMMBop," "Madeline," "I Will Come to You," and a medley of Christmas tunes from *Snowed In.* The *Meet Hanson* special also allowed the guys to show some of their acting prowess, as they pretended to star in and then be totally repulsed by remakes of scenes from classically corny Andy Williams 1970s Christmas specials. *Meet Hanson* worked on two levels—it showed Hanson as *the* sound of the late 1990s while recognizing their influences from past pop and rock leaders.

Hanson's first network TV special was followed two weeks later by the group's stints as musical guest on *Saturday Night Live* and the *Late Show with David Letterman.*

Of course, all of this tube exposure has led fans to hope that Hanson will soon star in its own TV series. (Imagine having a regularly scheduled half hour with Hanson every week!) But don't bet on it. As Ike explains, "We don't want to be the next Partridge Family. Right now, we're focusing on our music."

That kind of talk doesn't keep producers from trying to get Hanson on a TV series, however. "People have offered us sitcoms, but obviously we've turned them all down."

So much for the little screen. But what about the big screen? Are the Hanson hunks heading for a theater near you anytime soon? Well, it depends on whom you talk to. What is known for sure is that Hanson has rejected an idea to star in the big-screen remake of the '60s TV series *My Three Sons.* What is not known for certain is whether or not an actual Hanson bio-flick is in the works, one in which the boys would play themselves. The Hanson camp will neither confirm nor deny rumors that the movie is in preproduction, but magazines such as *Entertainment Weekly* have already disclosed that writer/director Morgan J. Freeman has been hired to write the screenplay, which will be heavily influenced by the Beatles' first flick, *A Hard Day's Night*. The comparisons are easy (even if Ike doesn't like to hear them). The opening scene of *A Hard Day's Night* shows the Beatles being chased through the streets of London by throngs of adoring, shouting, and crying female fans.

And what about Ike's life *out* of the public eye? He is a junior in high school now, and he'll soon have to start thinking about college. Ike would like to attend college someday, but he's realistic enough to know that he may have to put it off for a while to stick with Hanson. Still, he's not taking any chances. He's traveling with a math tutor these days, to make sure his numbers skills are up to snuff should he decide to take the SAT college entrance exams.

But no matter what Ike decides to do in adulthood, he's ready for the challenge. "It's all very much a learning experience," Ike says of growing up. "With every experience, you try to learn a little bit more about what you're doing and just try to do your job better."

One thing's for sure, Isaac Hanson's future will include being in the music business. And Ike hopes that as the years go by and he, Tay, and Zac grow older, people will stop thinking of them as kiddie pop performers.

"We're not a novelty act, and we don't plan to be," he insists passionately. "I know people say that about us. But we love making music, and we love what we're doing. We love where we are, and we want to keep doing it for the rest of our lives."

Besides composing and performing, Isaac wants to teach music and to produce music for Hanson and other artists. With Ike behind the controls, there's sure to be a musical future we can all look forward to!

16

THE ULTIMATE ISAAC HANSON POP QUIZ

So you think you know all there is to know about Hanson's fast-fingered guitar man, Ike? Well, maybe you do. But then again, maybe you *don't*. Take this Ike trivia test and find out. Some of the answers to the questions can be found within the pages of this book. But some of the questions can be answered only by the fans who like Ike the most! And just in case one or two of these questions stump you (and some are so tough, even Tay and Zac may not know the answers, so don't feel bad), you can check your answers on pages 75–77.

1. Is Ike left-handed or right-handed?
2. True or false: Ike is a senior in high school.
3. Which of Ike's parents plays the guitar?
4. What does Ike name his guitars after?

5. Who are Ike's best friends?
6. What is Isaac's favorite color?
   A. blue B. green C. yellow
7. True or false: Taylor has nicknamed Ike "Luke Skywalker" after his favorite character in *Star Wars*.
8. Which song has Ike singing lead on the *Middle of Nowhere* CD?
9. Which of these shows is *not* one of Ike's favorites?
   A. *Seinfeld* B. *Beavis and Butt-head* C. *Frasier* D. *Teen Angel*
10. True or false: Ike wrote his first song when he was eight years old.
11. True or false: *Snowed In* was recorded in Los Angeles.
12. Ike once composed a lullaby called "I'll Show You Mars" for whom?
13. To which magazine did Ike say, "You should interview us more often"?
    A. *Rolling Stone* B. *People* C. *Seventeen*
14. For which school subject does Ike have a tutor?
    A. literature B. math C. science
15. Where did Isaac get his first guitar?
16. What is the name of the first official Hanson song ever written?
    A. "Rain Falling Down" B. "If Ever I Saw Your Face" C. "MMMBop"
17. Why did Hanson have to play in the parking lot of the Blue Rose Cafe?

18. What did Rosie O'Donnell call Ike, Tay, and Zac?

19. What famous model do Ike and his brothers meet up with in *Tulsa, Tokyo, and the Middle of Nowhere?*

20. With whom does Ike trade off lead vocals on "Madeline"?

21. About which city did Ike marvel, "Everything is so tall, and it's all in this tiny area"?
A. Chicago B. Tokyo C. New York

22. From which state does Hanson come?

23. What is Ike's star sign?

24. True or false: Ike played a set of tennis against Martina Hingis at the Arthur Ashe Kids Day event in Queens, New York.

25. What instrument besides guitar does Ike play?

26. True or false: Hanson wrote the "Rockin' Around the Christmas Tree" track on *Snowed In.*

27. True or false: Isaac told photographers to forget it when they asked him to pose with a pile of stuffed animals.

28. True or false: There is soon to be a new Hanson.

29. Which of these sports is not one of Ike's faves?
A. street hockey B. surfing C. Rollerblading

30. True or false: At one time, the Hanson family owned six cats.

31. True or false: Once in a while, Ike likes to braid his hair.
32. True or false: Ike admits to getting nervous before going on TV.
33. What kind of novel has Isaac been working on for the past two years?
    A. a sci-fi novel B. a historical adventure that takes place during the Civil War C. A book about a rock band made up of brothers
34. Who wrote the "Everybody Knows the Claus" track on *Snowed In?*
35. What nickname has Ike given Zac?
36. Which of the following groups was *not* an influence on Hanson?
    A. The Beach Boys B. New Kids on the Block C. The Beatles
37. Which Hudson brother coproduced *Snowed In* with Hanson?
    A. Bill B. Mark C. Brett
38. Who are the executive producers on *Snowed In?*
39. True or false: Ike sings lead on "Where's the Love."
40. Which is the correct spelling?
    A. "MmBop" B. "MMMMBop"
    C. "MMMBop"
41. What is Ike's middle name?
42. True or false: Shock rocker Ozzy Osbourne is a huge fan of Hanson.
43. True or false: Ike once got locked in the house during a twister.

44. What was the name of the second Hanson album?
45. On what network did the "Cooking with Hanson" spots first appear?
46. Whom did morning TV anchor Katie Couric try to coax onstage during Hanson's *Today* show appearance?
47. What color are Ike's eyes?
48. Is Ike's hair naturally curly?
49. In what state was *Middle of Nowhere* recorded?
50. True or false: Ike likes to drag fans up onstage and dance with them.

ANSWERS TO THE ULTIMATE ISAAC HANSON POP QUIZ

1. Right-handed.
2. False. He's a junior.
3. His father.
4. Girls he likes.
5. His brothers Taylor and Zac.
6. B.
7. False. Isaac's nickname is "Chewbacca."
8. "Minute Without You."
9. D.
10. True.
11. False. It was recorded in England.

12. His youngest brother, Mackenzie.
13. C.
14. B.
15. At a pawn shop.
16. A.
17. Because it was a bar, and the boys were too young to go inside.
18. Real cutie patooties!
19. Cindy Crawford.
20. Taylor.
21. C.
22. Oklahoma.
23. Scorpio.
24. False. Hanson performed on the stage, but Ike never performed on the court.
25. He plays piano.
26. False. It was written by Johnny Marks.
27. True. He was afraid it would make people think of Hanson as a cute, teeny-bopper band, instead of the awesome musicians they really are.
28. It's true. Ike's mom, Diana, is pregnant with the seventh Hanson honey!
29. B.
30. True. It was just after their cat had five kittens.
31. False. It's Zac who likes braids.
32. False.
33. A.
34. Hanson.

35. "Animal," after the Muppets character that's always going wacko.
36. B.
37. B.
38. Hanson.
39. False.
40. C.
41. Isaac.
42. False. But his daughter is!
43. False. Even though Tulsa is definitely torna-do country, the Hanson brothers have yet to experience one . . . knock wood!
44. *MMMBop*.
45. Nickelodeon, as part of the SNICK block of programming.
46. Jessica, Avery, and Mackenzie. (She was unsuccessful.)
47. Dark brown.
48. Yes.
49. California.
50. False. It's Zac who has a past history of dragging fans up onstage.

YOUR SCORE

40–50 correct: You are a total Ike-head! Are you sure you weren't hiding in his suitcase as Hanson traveled the world?

25–39 correct: Your knowledge of Ike is awesome! Keep up the good work.

11–24 correct: An average score. But, since Ike is no average guy, maybe you'd better study up on him.

0–10 correct: Where have you been the past year—in the Middle of Nowhere?

17

IKE ON THE NET

If you have any doubt that Hanson is the most popular pop group on the entire planet, check out the World Wide Web. There are so many Web sites devoted to the brothers H that it would take you whole days to go through them all. People *are* going to all those Web sites, especially the official Hanson site (www.hansonline.com), which is receiving more than one million hits a month! Ike says, "We went from getting five e-mails a week to more than seven hundred!"

So where do you go if you want to know more about your favorite Hanson (which obviously is Ike)? Here are some Isaac Hanson Web sites to check out. But be prepared, Web sites come and go, so some of these may no longer be available by the time you check them out.

http://www.angelfire.com/ok/AlbertanesPage/
IkeInfo.html

http://members.aol.com/fowlersgrl/isaacbio.html

http://members.aol.com/TaylorHLRV/
IsaacHanson.html

http://www.angelfire.com/me/Hanson/overland/
ike.html

http://www.angelfire.com/va/hansondevotion/
page2.html

http://members.aol.com/FRGTMENOT/isaac.html

http://www.angelfire.com/ca/hansonpage/Isa.html

Now, there is a possibility that you'd like to
read about the other Hanson bros as well (and
who wouldn't? Tay and Zac are awfully hot in
their own rights). So, here are some general
Hanson Web sites you might want to take a look
at:

http://www.hansonhitz.com

http://www.polygram.com/mercury/artists/
hanson/hanson_homepage.html

http://www.geocities.com/Eureka/6540/

http://members.aol.com/Crescent14/hlink.html

http://members.aol.com/GSquiggles/
hansonfacts.html

But *don't* head over to the site at
http://www.hanson.com. This is *not* the Web site

of the Hanson music group. It's a business that happens to have the same name.

You already know that Ike is the ultimate techno teen. He loves anything with buttons, and that includes computers. Ike has been known to surf the Net. So if you really want to reach Ike, send him an e-mail. You might get a response. You never know!

And if you're not on-line yet, don't sweat it. You can still get all the hot news about Ike Hanson (and Tay and Zac, too, of course). Just send your name and address along with a stamped, self-addressed #10 envelope to

HITZ list,
PO Box 703136
Tulsa, OK 74170

About the Author

Nancy E. Krulik is a freelance writer who has previously written books on Ike's brother Taylor Hanson, pop stars New Kids on the Block, rap stars M.C. Hammer and Vanilla Ice, and teen actors the Lawrence brothers. She's also written for several Nickelodeon television shows. She lives in Manhattan with her husband and two children (who *love* Hanson).

Make sure you have the bestselling Hanson books with all the info on Taylor, Isaac, and Zac, each with eight pages of color photos!

MMMBop to the Top

By Jill Matthews

TOTALLY TAYLOR!

By Nancy Krulik

TOTALLY ZAC!

By Matt Netter

TOTALLY IKE!

By Nancy Krulik

Available now from Archway Paperbacks
Published by Pocket Books